CW01656588

THE KAMA SUTRA FOR SENIOR CITIZENS

The KAMA SUTRA *for* SENIOR CITIZENS

AND OTHER POEMS ON AGING

ZACK ROGOW

VP

VALLEY PRESS

First published in 2026 by Valley Press
Woodend, The Crescent, Scarborough, UK, YO11 2PW
valleypressuk.com

ISBN 978-1-915606-69-3
Cat. no. VP0256

Copyright © Zack Rogow 2026

The right of Zack Rogow to be identified as the author of this work has been asserted in accordance with the Copyright, Designs and Patents Act 1988.

All rights reserved. No part of this publication may be reproduced, stored in or introduced into a retrieval system, or transmitted in any form, by any means (electronic, mechanical, photocopying, recording or otherwise) without prior written permission from the rights holders.

Cover and text design by Jamie McGarry.
Title poem illustration by Ilse Gordon.

Contents

for Esta, with love and admiration

12
9
3
6
BYRON
COLETTE
KAMA
Sutra
Seniors

The *Kama Sutra* for Senior Citizens

Don't worry
if you can't do all the moves:
"twining the vine,"
that standing position,

or "the peacock's foot" – indents
that fingernails leave on skin,

or the love scratches
called "the blue lotus."

Don't get stuck on bite marks:
either "the coral and jewels"
or "the broken cloud."

It's not necessary for the *yoni* to grip the *lingam*
in "the pair of tongs."

The *auparishtaka* or "mouth congress":
yes, that's one possibility,
also "the stag and the doe,"
but keep in mind

that any time you can still go crazy enough to come
it's a benediction of the flesh,
if it's with another, or
with your own knowledgeable touch,

and even if you can't anymore,
there are more types of passion
than peaks in the Himalayas.

The Muse Answers an Old Poet

Sing to you *again*?
You gotta be kidding, old man!
I've already inspired your viscous love lyrics
for decades. You want me
to serenade you at *your* age,
when your bald pate is mottled
as camouflage? When your wool scarf is
looped around your neck
even in spring sunshine,
and you can't even
remember the *title* of the book
you read last month?

If you write anything now
shouldn't it be codicils
that list who should get your belongings,
and a directive on when to yank the plug?

My calendar's a ladder
of *young* writers now,
authors whose work comes out
in hardcover. It's strictly softcover
at your age, grandpa! But I see

from your sorry first drafts
you still have a heart
that yearns for pillow talk
and eloquent caresses.

Oh, alright! Maybe
I'll warble for you one last time.
At least you still remember
this muse isn't just cello curves –
I'm actually a goddess.
Well, to be honest, I'm a little of both.

After a Friend's Diagnosis

When you grow old you have to say goodbye
to shallots, leeks, and their poor relations –
onions and garlic;
also chilis, poblanos, and ghost peppers;
a Michelangelo of a burger
with all the toppings;
cold golden champagne and its bright bubbles;
real sugar real butter real everything.

Uh huh, let it all go:
the hike on a narrow mountain trail with a steep
drop-off to a chiseled valley;
the dream of hearing birdsong in the rainforest
while lying on a rope bed
scrimmed in mosquito netting;

not to mention your dearest friends
dwindling one by one,
those rare humans who care deeply
about all the precious nonsense you love:
a walk-off, inside-the-park home run;
or Bill Evans leaning 90 degrees
over the ivories as he breaks your heart
playing "Who Can I Turn To?"

What My Mother Told Me at the Automat

for my mother, Mickey Rogow (1919–1972)

When I was just barely double digits,
you had to bribe me
into buying crunchy new school clothes
by promising me a lunch break
at the Horn & Hardart Automat.

Inside, everything was streamlined
as the set of an old Hollywood musical.
Polished chrome framed little windows
each containing a dish
of Salisbury steak and mashed potatoes,
or an arc of apple pie,
or the dreaded creamed spinach.

A cashier made change from red paper rolls
of new nickels bright as headlights,
the currency that magically
liberated the food.

In that dining hall,
sibilant with a hundred conversations,
you were appareled as ever
in a tightly tailored dress
and platinum bracelets.
You spoke to me of so many things:

never start smoking (as you
lit up yet another unfiltered cigarette);
wrong, wrong, the contorted souls
who hate whole groups of people;
and remember, you said,
sex is actually good,
and don't let anyone tell you otherwise.

You opened all those little windows for me,
onto a world
that I still only glimpsed
in the unpolished distance,
some of it cinnamon-sweet,
and some of it even much worse
than creamed spinach.

What My Mother Never Told Me

Widowed in your early thirties,
you still had those Venus legs
and a pair of high heels to match
each of your darted dresses.
The eyes of the husbands in your circle must have
tracked you closely.

I wonder about that time
you took me and my sister
to stay at that little, out-of-the-way hotel
overlooking the Seine.
Who should turn up in Paris
but the father of the family
we joined for turkey dinners,
his spouse and kids
nowhere to be seen?

And what about that trip to Madrid,
where we met a tall Louisiana executive
taking his young son to the bullfights.
He changed hotels
to stay on the same floor as you.
You certainly had a way

with the gentlemen,
your lit cigarette dangling
between two fingers
and that irrepressible laugh.
It tumbled in dark waves, your hair,
setting off those hazel eyes
and elevated cheekbones.

Your kittenish voice led no one
to expect your strong statements
on civil rights and peace.

Who could you confide in
about your Bette Davis affairs in foreign capitals
that sometimes left you
crying on the airplane back home,
to my infinite, pre-teen shame?
Who could you tell about
a trip to the moon on gossamer wings –
just one of those things,
that Cole Porter/Frank Sinatra ballad
you spun on vinyl over and over.

If you had lived longer, Mums,
you could tell *me* now,
though you chose to burn out quickly
like a chrysanthemum firework.
You could tell me
all about those white nights,
because God knows
you're the one who could best understand
how much my heart takes after yours.

Short Stay: To My Ex

Do you remember that hotel
where we stayed just an afternoon
finding new ways to braid our limbs
till I felt my soul had a twin,

and the front desk clerk, knowing
that only lovers check out at five p.m.
comped us the room
so we bought him four grinning sunflowers.

If I choose to remember that day
and not just those years when –
unable to resist gravity –
we lasered each other with insult after insult

then will you pardon me for reminding you
of those soft memories
since the arc of our love
also touches that blinding midday
at the sunflower hotel
and not just the unnumbered nights
when we lay side by side
meticulously avoiding all touch.

No One Congratulates You

No one congratulates you.
No one throws you a party
with mirrory invitations.
You don't get to try on a floor-length gown
or a new jet tux.
No marquise-cut diamond
or 14-carat halo on your finger.
No shower to open *ooh* and *aah* packages,
or a frou-frou gâteau several layers high
with just one figure on the top.
You hear no toasts over bubbles and smiles,
sacerdotal blessings,
Pachelbel on the buzz-cut lawn,
or sendoffs to a colada destination.

When you end a relationship,
no one congratulates you.
All you get is the fragrant ozone of freedom,
and shadows growing ever longer.

BUMPERSTICKERS

MY OTHER CAR IS A CHAIN SMOKER

MY OTHER CAR RESEMBLES A 1936 PLATINUM
CIGARETTE CASE

MY OTHER CAR IS AN AGING MUPPET

MY OTHER CAR SPEAKS SANSKRIT WITH A HINT
OF A POLISH ACCENT

MY OTHER CAR HAS A CRUSH ON YOUR OTHER
CAR

MY OTHER CAR PLAYED HAMLET IN COLLEGE

MY OTHER CAR RUNS ON FREE VERSE POETRY

MY OTHER CAR IS PRESOCRATIC

MY OTHER CAR THINKS IN TOPOLOGY

MY OTHER CAR WAS AN ABSTRACT
EXPRESSIONIST BUT HAS SINCE REPENTED

MY OTHER CAR IS AN HONOR STUDENT AT
CARDINAL NEWMAN MIDDLE SCHOOL

MY OTHER CAR WOULD RATHER BE SURFING

HONK IF YOU LIKE MY OTHER CAR

WHAT WOULD JESUS DO IN MY OTHER CAR

MY OTHER CAR FOR PRESIDENT

MY OTHER CAR ASPIRES TO UNIVERSALITY

LET'S FACE IT MY OTHER CAR IS BARELY ON
SPEAKING TERMS WITH THIS CAR

Two Types of People in This World

There are two types of people:
the ones who tuck in their sheets every morning and the ones
  who don't bother,
those who think their pets are gods and those who beg to differ,
the smokers and the fanners of cigarettes,
the ones who antennify an invisible divine current,
and the I-don't-think-so's,
those who believe in the constellations,
and those who believe in numbers,
TV watchers, TV teetotalers,
rule makers rule breakers,
the few who remember punchlines and the rest who just laugh,
people who think the planet is steadily rolling upwards,
and those who toss another empty onto the rising pile,
the poor fools who live for passion,
and the poor fools who don't.

Body Snatcher

When I look in the mirror
I think of that 1950s horror flick
Invasion of the Body Snatchers,
where a giant seed pod
hidden in a suburban greenhouse
bubbles till it becomes a double of you,
and that alien, at first half
vegetable and half human,
twangs into motion
and takes over your life.

But who is this impostor
so much older than I am,
with his domed head,
a bushy body and paunch
mushrooming each month,
his hands and head so variegated
no suntan can disguise the spots.

How did that geezer
slip into my house
and impersonate me,
grabbing my name,
my friends, my children,
pretending he *is* me,
and that he's writing
this poem.

There Are Nights When You Forget How to Sleep

There are nights when you forget how to sleep,
forget how to dream even recurring dreams with their
inescapable rooms,
nights you forget how to lie in bed.

There are nights when no prayer or mantra will calm the brain's
electrical storm,
when you remember slaps not slow-motioned by forgiveness,
remember sticky songs impossible to shake off,
pleasures held and withheld,
remember how you could have done more for your loved ones
and for the cauliflower gradually going gray in the refrigerator.

There are nights when it seems you'll never sleep again
so you fold back the sheet and the heavy blanket
and rise at an hour greater than one
and less than five
to perform the penance
of reading a glacial book or returning each dish to its home –
until you finally lie down again
resigned to attempt the impossible task of resting
and without your knowing how
sleep finally slips in
through the one door you left unguarded.

Nostalgic for Tragedy

Unseemly for a poet
to live a long life,
to gather white hair and grandkids,
long-term hubby or wife.

A poet should go young
in a snap and tragic death,
in the drink like Shelley
or an overdose of meth.

Consumption's a fitting path,
e.g., Keats in Rome,
or smashed in a crash
with glass and steel and chrome;

or like those crystal souls,
say Sexton or Berryman,
who row their own way
to Charon, the ferryman.

And don't forget Chatterton,
"the marvellous boy,"
who glugged down the arsenic.
Oy yoy yoy yoy yoy!

A short life shines bright
as a big burp of lava –
think Rimbaud in Africa,
smuggling guns and java.

I've waited so long, though,
for firing squad or goring
that it's too late to die young:
I'll just have to die boring.

Senior Moments

WHEN YOU'RE OLDER

the moon
increases from
just a nail clipping
to a full thumbprint
faster than fingers
can snap.

OUT OF REACH

I've forgotten what a forget-me-not looks like.

4:00 A.M.

lying in bed
when it's no longer night
but not yet morning
such a pleasant dream I had
and can't quite recall.

BLESS THE DOCTORS

These days, I have more doctors than friends.

THIS BUSINESS OF GETTING OLD

This business of getting old gets old pretty fast.

MILESTONE

You reach a point in your life
where you hope you'll be outlived
by your car.

GRAY

The grayer your hair gets,
the less you see the world as just black and white.

The New Hip

If I live long enough I'll
have a walker with wheels
and move cautiously
like an airplane
taxiing on the tarmac

The Hand of Aging Touches Some Gently

The hand of aging touches some gently,
lovingly smoothing cheekbones,
forehead rotundas,
and the ogives of eyes.

For others, the hand of aging
sucker punches them in the gut.
Use all the oxygen creams
and hair balayage you want:

sometimes genes just have their way.
The men on my father's side
inherit knees that give out after sixty
like branches overstocked with snow.

Seconds, minutes, hours, days:
clocks have the hungriest jaws.
Days, weeks, months, years:
life has no clickable Pause.

Pumping Gas in Central Point, Oregon

Excuse me, sorry, state law!
You can't pump the gas yourself here in Oregon.

You want me to top it off with premium?

See from your plates you're from California.
You've collected enough bugs on that windshield
to start a museum. I'll clean it for you.

You here for Shakespeare?
Lotta people drive up for the festival.

Where you from in California?

Really? I was born right near there,
before the yuppies and the hipsters moved in
and the prices went to outer space.
So I moved up here.
Plenty of folks in Oregon
hair gray as mine.

Don't speed, now.
The cops don't even bother
with sirens anymore.
They pop a picture
and the ticket arrives in the mail
like you ordered it online.

Shouldn't chew your ear off.
You got someplace to go.

Thank you, sir. I appreciate it.
You know I used to pump gas
when I was a teenager.
Never thought I'd still be doing this
at my age.

Confessions of Methuselah

How long have I lived? So long
I've seen slingshots change to fiery missiles
that burned Persepolis to the ground.
I've witnessed floodwaters
carry off bronze temple doors,
and warm cottages abolished
so they could raise towers
with shadows that race across the square.

People now dress in less than undergarments.
Who even cares?
Only Methuselah. Yes, I stare
but they don't notice.
And if they do, they yell,
"What are you looking at,
you old schnauzer?"
Go ahead, laugh at this
dried-up fig.

Is the flash of youth
worth an old age lasting centuries?
Now I barely remember
when I was spry enough
to fling a javelin
one hundred cubits
and plant it trembling
in the wet ground.

But I've walked in cities bright
with ten thousand sconces
where once there was only an ocean of sand.
I watched fringe heresies become gospel.
And I got to laugh with men and women
who now are legend.

Where Are They Now?

We tracked down renowned figures in the history of philosophy, spirituality, and science and found out what they are doing today.

PLATO has started a chain of clothing outlets that sells only the Platonic idea of a garment. The prices are quite reasonable.

ARCHIMEDES finally found a lever and a place to stand on, and moved the world. He's now retired and lives in Boca Raton, Florida.

LAO TZU has opened a Museum of Non-Being, featuring a hundred different voids. Visitors are chosen at random, and members are forbidden to enter.

BUDDHA is working anonymously at a famous chocolate maker in Paris, trying to determine if he may have overstated the case when he said, "All life is suffering."

JOAN OF ARC has reluctantly admitted she's an Anglophile and is now binge-watching *The Crown*.

TOMÁS DE TORQUEMADA, founder of the Spanish Inquisition, was convicted of forty-three counts of tax fraud and is serving the sixth of his twelve consecutive 99-year sentences in a Turkish prison.

VOLTAIRE is cultivating his garden and is eager for tips on how to protect against cabbage slugs.

ADAM SMITH is now a real estate developer of gated communities for retired despots. He is said to be investing heavily in Siberian tundra because of rising global temperatures.

Friedrich Nietzsche is currently a recluse living in a shepherd's stone cottage in the Slovenian Alps. In a rare interview, he revealed that he now eats mostly eggplant and enjoys online Zumba classes.

Karl Marx joined a band of guerrillas in the jungles of Colombia, where he became intrigued by organic farming. He is currently part of a collective that grows açai fruit for the health food market.

Friedrich Engels organized workers for many years in a chicken processing plant in the former East Germany, where he was able to improve safety measures, though not for the chickens. He now takes care of his great-great-great-granddaughter, picking her up at daycare.

Albert Einstein is the CEO of a startup that hopes to extend longevity by sending one of a pair of identical twins into space at nearly the speed of light.

George Washington Carver invented edible takeout containers made from sweet potatoes. After use, the containers can be heated into a delicious soup. Carver recommends adding oyster mushrooms, Tuscan kale, and silken tofu.

Simone de Beauvoir and Jean-Paul Sartre have become fascinated by competitive cycling and have started an all-gender, non-Eurocentric alternative to the Tour de France, located in South America and ending at Machu Picchu.

Martin Heidegger is a bagger in a supermarket in West Terre Haute, Indiana, and has been heard muttering, "What is the meaning of Being?" to random customers. He also watches Hoosier football on TV, but only road games.

Mahatma Gandhi is designing a line of eyeglasses and walking sticks called Gandhiware, based on his signature accessories. All proceeds will be donated to promote marine mammal literacy.

Ayn Rand lost all her savings and her health insurance when her investments in mortgage-backed securities tanked in the Great Recession of 2008. She is now cleaning rooms in a chain motel in Galveston, Texas, and is still a firm believer in the free market.

Mother Teresa is hoping to launch a string of nightclubs where participants dance in separate rooms to music that no one else is hearing. Rumor has it that she is not finding much venture capital.

I Don't Know How to Grow Old

I have no role model for aging:
my mother and father left at intermission,
and I barely knew their parents.

All except Grandpa Abe
who challenged me to a race
when he was too old to run
and I was too young to forgive
his thinking he could win.
At least Abe ate lots of "wedge-it-a-bulls,"
a good role model for fiber intake,
if nothing else.

How to grow old
without pitying my hands, without
becoming as repetitive as an on-hold phone message?
How to "Good Morning!" the mirror?

Once I met a man who'd just celebrated his 99th birthday,
his mind clear as an aquarium,
his body lean as a tuna.
I asked him his secret. He told me,
"I chew my food 50 times before swallowing."
I thought:
I'm not that good a human being.

My sister's mother-in-law,
an actress who kept her Oscar on top of the TV –
I idolized her –
but when she aged she recited
over and over the lines
Who stole my keys?
Who stole my keys? –
a particular ring of hell.

I don't know how to grow old
but it seems my body does.
Now I'm the one saying,
Where are my glasses?
What's my password again?
And what happened to all those people I once loved?

— INTERMISSION —

For Yoshiko Uchida

Based on a story told to me by the U.S. writer Yoshiko Uchida (1921–1992)

Not long after World War II,
when Japan was still rebuilding
its cities and its identity,
the young writer Yoshiko Uchida
went back to the country of her parents' birth
to study with the great potter, Shoji Hamada.

A question for her mentor
mosquitoed her for months,
but she held back on asking, afraid
it would offend him.
Just before leaving for home,
she watched the agèd artist glaze
a ripe red line near the lip
of a new black bowl,
and she summoned the courage:
"Master Hamada, why
don't you ever sign your pots?
You have so many imitators.
How are they going to tell your work apart in the future?"

Hamada squinted at his bowl. "My worst work
will be attributed to my imitators."
He turned to gaze at the young woman
through his circular spectacles
with their black rims.
"Their best work
will be attributed to me."

For Chaim Soutine

(1893–1943)

On a good day, one chicken wing,
a beet, and some gruel.
His father, a tailor,
supported eleven children
by patching worn *schmattes*.
The tenth-born was Chaim.

Smilovichi – the Belarus shtetl where he grew up,
a blank space
on most maps.
Only seven years old,
Chaim sold his *mammele*'s one good kitchen knife
to buy colored crayons.
Two days locked in the colorless cellar
to pay for his crime.
Lacking paper, he drew
on houses and walls,
sketched the local rabbi,
whose son thrashed him –
"Don't. Make. Graven. Images!"

At twenty, Soutine arrived in Paris.
Before looking for a room,
he took his leaky suitcase
straight to the Musée du Louvre.
The museum became his mentor.
His studio at *La Ruche*, The Hive.
Soutine downed carafes
of cheap red Rhône with Chagall
and the other artists of the Jewish Montparnasse.
Modigliani dubbed him
"the greatest painter of the twentieth century."

Soutine fidgeted across rural *paysages*,
one of the few artists gifted
at both landscapes and portraits,
his brushwork of trees
hallucinatory with motion.
He used to buy back his old canvases from galleries
and slash them to strips
to punish his mistakes.

The eyes he painted – they incubated stories –
a childlike businessman,
choirboys praying
for temptation, the sweet
twisted whimsy of the *Woman in Red*.
When all he had left was a herring,
he painted a herring.

A collector once offered him a thousand francs
for a landscape he'd never seen.
Soutine flung the bills to the gutter.

Chaim eluded the Gestapo
only to die of a punctured intestine.
And now, of course, his work in every MoMA.

What kind of life is this
where there's almost never justice for artists
until they become a tombstone?
Still, I'd like to propose a toast:
L'chaim. To Chaim.
To life.

Lord Byron to His Daughter Ada

Missolonghi, Greece, 12th April 1824

My dearest daughter, no doubt you ponder
How you came to have a father reviled
By the press, gossips, your mother; who'd squander
His choicest of years, from England exiled
To Venice and Ravenna, to wander
And never glimpse how time has changed his child.
So I'm sending you, my señorita,
This *apologia pro sua vita*.

Accusers say I chase every passion,
Boy or girl; that gaming I just accrue
Mont Blancs of debt; my gilded coach I fashion
After Bonaparte's; sired a child or two
On the side; no pleasure do I ration.
It well could be that every word is true!
I hope those who claim I'm the fount of all evil
Concede at least I'm a handsome devil.

"Most selfish writer who e'er walked the earth."
Aye, that's I, they blabber of no other.
And yet I sailed to Greece, to midwife the birth
Of a country free and united, mother
Of gods and soft marble – for all that's worth.
Each faction would rather knife the other.
With fever freezing, at thirty-six my life
May end before I see an end to their strife.

I’ve heard that you have quite a head for maths –
From *moi* you could have never gained that skill.
All children should stumble toward their own paths
Leave parents’ dreams for parents to fulfill.
My absence I won’t excuse, nor calm your wraths.
You felt them when I left, you feel them still.
But a poet for a parent – you could do worse.
You never knew your father – you’ll know him from his verse.

Photos I Appear in by Chance

I'm the slurred figure in the background
of the selfie the honeymooners took
near the Rialto Bridge in Venice.
The home movie that gobbled the whole panorama
of the Grand Canyon in summer
ends with me at age 22,
dazed and dehydrated
dragging myself up from the Colorado River Valley.
I'm the pop-eyed passerby
that a guy deliberately captured on film
after his girlfriend peeled off her t-shirt
on a deserted street in San Francisco.
And that's me
behind the family group portrait,
strolling by as I *whap!* a mosquito on my forehead.

How many unnumbered albums and videos do I appear in
belonging to people I'll never meet –
the closest I'll ever get
to immortality.

— PLEASE RETURN TO YOUR SEATS —

Senior's Dating Site Profile

We all have baggage; I hope yours has wheels.

I'm an ex-New Yorker, but I can still taste when a bagel hasn't been boiled. I'm also a fitness and health buff, but to be honest, my shot put and discus throw are a little rusty.

Like everyone, I'm looking for a person with a sense of humor: gold, silver, and bronze for irony, sarcasm, and dry wit.

I'm a hugger, I hope you are too.

Solo a Venezia

The sloshing boats at night on the *Canal Grande*,
the blue thread of daylight at the end
of a narrow waterway,
the *palazzi* with their honeycomb windows
and their pointed arches like the negative
space under hands in prayer – strange
not to share these with anyone,
to be alone here in Venice.

Odd to wander this
labyrinth all day,
not part of the world
of couples posing together
for selfies on the Rialto,
trading licks of amaretto gelato,
or lifting strollers up and down,
and up and down
the marble bridges.

And if one night
I pass another solitary face
and we exchange an unmasked glance,
I wonder if she might be the one
who would fancy a minotaur,
the woman who could also find
a minotaur's cave.

Half a Century of Sex

Upside down and backwards,
traveling every moist passageway
from every possible approach,
licking and kissing and sucking
from earlobes to toes.

And, oh my God! –
the smells –
fish sauce,
dulse,
and overripe double cream.

On the balcony beyond midnight
above tropical tides,
at dawn in a flat near the Champs-Élysées,
in the office as the carillon belled midday,
oral in the forest
right before the Boy Scouts marched by,
ravenous as a pack of wild dogs,
or gentle as cat fur.

And now, looking back,
I ask myself:
is it *enough* already?
Well, almost.

The Ocean, for Example

What does the ocean do
when it creates a failure
of a wave, a mangy little billow
that fizzles onto the shore,
a dud that never goes beyond
muddled ruffles?
What does the ocean do then?

It makes another wave.

And what does the ocean do
when it spins a perfect turquoise
Murano wave,
a liquid aqua cylinder
flawlessly unfurling?
What does the ocean do then?

I think you already know.

Bird in Flight

Charlie Parker with Strings*, the saxophonist's classic album, was released in 1950.*

I understand now
why Charlie Parker took one look
at the string orchestra assembled to record behind him –
the curvaceous violins,
the Steinway grand
shiny as a ball gown,
and the harp strings
shimmering with anticipation –
I can understand why he took one glance
at his lifelong dream of that ensemble
and walked right out the door.

When they finally found Bird
ten days later and asked him why,
he said, "It was so beautiful."

Yes, I understand
now that I'm at last alone with you
in this city
with its lantern skyscrapers,
each of us having spent years learning
how to love,
and how *not* to love,
so close to you now
I can understand Charlie Parker's flight
because this *is* so beautiful
that I want to rush out the door
and run where no one can find me.

But I won't
because,
            bless his soul,
Charlie Parker already did that
for all of us.

Soggy Jazz

In memory of the chanteuse Denise Perrier (1939–2021)

Chilled in drizzly San Francisco
I listen to a quartet plus a warm voice
travel "On Green Dolphin Street"
in this store with alleys of books

The singer glides between the notes
teasing the melody

And through these moments apart
Mem'ries live in my heart

My thoughts glissando back an hour
when not even a sheet could
fit between us

The baritone sax with its extraterrestrial architecture
picks up the melody

Your tongue
a dolphin in an underwater cavern

I can't help weaving to the music
as the band starts to knit back together
the loose threads of the melody
saxophone notes shaping the air

Green Dolphin Street supplied the setting
The setting for nights beyond forgetting

and hours later
when I get home
and take off my meadow-colored pullover
its arms
still hold your perfume

The Map of Former Loves

At that seaside resort, you nested
with your ex. My first wife and I diagonaled up
this mountain right before our wedding
so she could squeeze into her dress.
In the bistro at that country crossroads you shared bites
of succulent mignon by candlelight
with a former flame.

At our age the geography of love becomes dense.
There are more Xs on our grids
than on a pirate's treasure map. Even to plan
a weekend away we have to zigzag
around scores of memories.

Some stumble upon their lifelong mate
before they can even vote.
I envy them,
the lucky ones who find platinum love
without having to wait.
But wait –
they didn't find you.

Other Times We Might Have Met

We might have met when we were seventeen,
when we didn't even know how it felt
to touch a body unlike our own.
We could've snuck from the floral sofa to your bedroom
while the parents were snoring
and spent the whole night
exploring new landscapes.

Or we could have met after college
when bosses and mortgages
were our treasured worries.
We might have made a child then
with your azurite eyes
and the soft, wiry brown hair
I still had in those years.

Or we could have encountered each other
right after our divorces
when our kids were puzzling
over algebraic expressions
or practicing jazz trombone.

We happened to meet now, though,
when the children have
scattered to their own homes,
when more about me is wrinkled
than my sheets, when our bodies still glow
with a beauty that once blazed.

But without having lived
through love gone sour,
would we have understood
how rare our meeting is,
like finding a beach stippled with scallop shells,
all split, chipped, cracked, crushed,
and then lifting one complete one
out of the sand,
and rinsing it in a clear sheet of water.

Alstroemeria

You sprouted Orange King alstroemeria from seeds
twenty-five years ago.
Gently you placed them
between strata of moist paper towels.
When shoots appeared you
poked them one by one into the soil.
They bloomed only once, and afterwards –
nothing.

Now, after two successive springs
fluent in rain,
they've suddenly ripvanwinkled.
Many blossoms
pop up from the ivy ground cover
eager as fledglings
greeting a parent bird bearing morsels.

I'm so glad that alstroemeria know
how to alchemize leaden skies
into golden petals
without any help from us
because our species is
far from nature's most dependable friend,
and long after we're gone, flowers will rise up
toward brightness and starlight
and the muck of puddles.

Domino Days

How a string of hours
makes a day,
and the days
crowd into months,
months domino
to years
years collide
into decades –
it's more
than I can fathom.

But if you'll sit close to me
by this cliff
and watch just one
sunset
over the
Tiffany
ocean
as the cirrus clouds
turn a powdery orange
against a sky
tincturing to violet
then I'll welcome
another day
yielding
its colors
to the night.

Museum Sells Chagall Painting to Buy Minimalist Art

It was possibly the worst decision
in the history of museum curating:
in 1990 the Guggenheim in New York
auctioned off Marc Chagall's *Birthday*
in order to buy Minimalist art.

It's that stunning Chagall,
where an armless, green-shirted man
floats across the room to kiss his astonished beloved,
although she's leaning so far into his lips
she might take off herself at any moment
or drop the bouquet she seems to be offering
to the little street outside their window.

The museum didn't call what they did to the Chagall "selling."
No, they labeled it "deaccessioning,"
a verbal crime almost as venal as the sale itself.

With substantial funds from that auction,
the Guggenheim bought a canvas
that resembled a giant sheet of graph paper,
and seven identical boxes
made of steel, and airbrushed a uniform orange.

I suppose the museum director
who made this brilliant decision
was embarrassed by the frank emotion of the Chagall,
by then a trope of modern art.

How quickly even the most
Jacobin images become
caricatures: Dalí's watch melting
like cheese on a burger;
Magritte's bowler upstaged by an apple;
Munch's wiggly, howling ghoul.

And it's true, feelings are so cliché –
flowers on a birthday?
Come *on*, Marc!
So it seems at first nearly
redundant for us to kiss when we're close,
we've done it many times,
on many sofas,
with many lovers,
and yet how quickly our hands fly
in ways that only lovers can endure.

Nietzsche's Idea of the Eternal Recurrence Applied to My Love Life

What if a demon were to sneak after you in your loneliest loneliness and say, "This life as you now live it and have lived it, you will have to live once more and innumerable times more ... even this spider and this moonlight between the trees."

– *Friedrich Nietzsche,* The Joyful Wisdom

Would I really want to relive it all, over and over?

My first love at thirteen, the one who
tossed me aside like a gum wrapper
for a "more sophisticated" fourteen-year-old –
how I wept!

All my unrequited phone messages
left for hopeless crushes
as numerous as love ballads
with their nectar of sadness.

The marriage I dashed into
because it was that time in life
and the in-laws treated me like their long-lost child.
Then the divorce
when those same in-laws forgot my name
and my children pinned it all on me.
Maybe rightly.

It was so painful the first time
but I'd embrace it all again and again
if it leads to this moment
when we both look back on our past lovers
alive or in ashes

and kiss each other that much firmer
and hold each other that much tighter
knowing we had to crawl across those battlefields
to wake together in a warm broth of daylight.

Elegy for a Therapist

in memory of Dr. Alla Volovich (1962–2021)

Right before I heard the news about you
I saw a tightrope walker
who had strung his cable across a gorge
and before I could take it all in he
fell headfirst
I held my breath
The tightrope walker
bounced back up
caught by his safety cord
He dangled upside down
like the tarot card The Hanged Man

You never told me much about yourself
so generously examining the thorns and thistles
I gathered for you every week
You accepted them like a bouquet
I didn't even know
you had a husband
the one who called to tell me
you drowned while diving
among eels and mushroom coral

You were not a *shrink*
You expanded
expanded my childhood
till I saw it in sharp focus for the first time
and the way it throbs in the present

Some days I walk a tightrope
I was so lucky
that for years
you were the safety cord

The Wrong Time to Bring a Child into This World

for my daughter Miranda

You tell me this is not the right time to bring a child into this world
and I also see glaciers melting like diamonds and the oceans
spilling over while brushfires sprint across hillsides
I see intensive care units with patients wrestling the air

I never wanted to bring a child into this world
until your mother insisted
she had to know the pain of parenting

until you lay in a clear plastic rectangle
in newborn intensive care
and I wanted more than anything
to bring you home
to the stuffed-animal mobile over your crib

until I heard your blue-streak three-year-old monologue
and I couldn't help laughing and kvelling

until I watched your turned-out arms-extended gait
so like your late mom's
and I saw her features
ripple across your face

Toddler at Grandma's

Mommy says I can play with anything I can reach so I'm
knocking down every single stacking block

Mommy still paying attention
Yes

Time to grab each plastic lid out of the cabinet and
fling it as far as I can

Mommy's watching
Perfect

Now I'm opening all the books on the shelf and flipping them
every which way
Grandma says No
don't throw the heavy ones with the color pictures
Too bad
Maybe when the Bigbigs aren't looking

Grandma takes me to look at the cookies baking in the don't-
touch
The cookies look like Mommy's eyes

But where is that Mommy
Nowhere I can see
I'm running into every room I'm starting to cry I'm even
looking in the bathroom
What is she doing in there without me

She's at the sink
I hug her leg tight as I can
She reaches down and lifts me
My cheek against her soft cheek
I smell that yummymommysmell
So good

OK   let me go now   let me go
I have to take all the metal pans out of the cupboards and crash them to the floor

Gus and the Sunbeam

One-year-old Gus
slaps the sofa cushion lying on the floor.
Dust motes flutter into the air,
scintillating in a late-afternoon sunbeam.

Gus wants to touch the churning motes,
but he can't reach them from the floor,
so he pulls himself up with the coffee table
and grabs a fistful of sparkles,
squinting at those flickers
that don't feel like anything.

But what makes the sunbeam?
He traces the light back
to the glass wall facing the deck.
Gus crawls over and raises himself up
against the transparent barrier,
stretches as tall as he can,
and tries to reach that orange circle beyond it.
He pounds and pounds his palm against the glass.
That thing is so bright, its beam is
right there in the living room,
why can't he touch it,
why can't he touch the sun?

Running through History

3:37
3:52

I realize
the treadmill's blinking numbers
that count minutes and seconds
could be years of history

4:10 I jog through the sack of Rome
6:18 the Tang Dynasty rises in China
The angel Gabriel whispers to Mohammed to write the Qur'an
7:11 I turn up the pace as the Moors pour into Andalusia
Troubadour Arnaut Daniel rides toward a Provençal hill town
playing air-lute
12:38 the Alhambra's delicate fortress ascends above Granada
A puzzled Geoffrey Chaucer glances up from his writing desk
I sprint right through the Great Vowel Shift
Into the greenery of Botticelli's *Primavera*
Deftly I step over the bubonic plague
14:53 Ottoman cannons breach Constantinople
Columbus sets sail; I race him to Hispaniola
The French Revolution breaks out to my left
18:21 Bolívar wins the Battle of Carabobo; the Spanish Empire
cracks
19:19 My parents are born
Plenipotentiaries sign the Treaty of Versailles
19:44 D-Day and then the year of my own birth almost before I
see it
I slow dance to "Mister Moonlight"
My first kiss
Crowds unbuild the Berlin Wall
I become a father
South Africans wave hankies for President Mandela
20:12 the Mars Rover cuts me off

The present day rushes by
Then the years I hope I'll live to count
My daughter stands beneath the chuppah
My unconceived grandchild laughs for the first time

I slow the treadmill
step off
and even though I'm not moving
I'm still running

Numerous

as the tabla beats of the raindrops
the legions of ants delighting in an open jar of honey
gold bubbles necklaced in a glass of champagne
a marathon of poppies racing over a hillside
the crackles of light on the bay
the integers lining up to catch a glimpse of infinity
stars powdering the night
the galaxies that form like embryos
the times I've given thanks that you and I are one couple

Polar Duplicates

You shove open all the windows
because you're always too warm
but I'm too cold
so I bang them shut again

Your fingers dig in the garden among twisting roots and dark loam
While my hands flutter across a silver laptop

You love to sleep under slowly spinning constellations
My idea of roughing it:
Central Park

I jounce right out of bed
You linger under the covers
flicking through your phone

"I like a Gershwin tune..."
and you like the Stones

I go for a lick of haiku
You gnaw through long French novels

You ride your bike up Mont Ventoux
I pay a call on my favorite
Delacroix in the Louvre

And yet we meet every night
by the pixel glow of the TV
side by side on the sofa
we gradually lean into one another
and our hands
shy strangers
edge closer and closer
till at last
they clasp

Acknowledgments

The author wishes to thank the editors of the following journals and anthologies for publishing poems from this collection:

Abandoned Mine Magazine: "The Hand of Aging Touches Some Gently" and "Toddler at Grandma's."

Aji Magazine: "The Ocean, for Example."

Arlington Literary Journal: "Confessions of Methuselah," and "Body Snatchers."

The Bombay Review (India): "For Yoshiko Uchida," "Pumping Gas in Central Point, Oregon."

Bronze Bird Review: "Photos I Appear in by Chance."

The Brussels Review (Belgium): "What My Mother Told Me at the Automat."

Coneflower Café: "Gus and the Sunbeam" (Finalist for Derick Burleson Poetry Prize), and "Nietzsche's Idea of the Eternal Return Applied to My Love Life."

Cirque: "Lord Byron to His Daughter Ada."

De la Mancha: "Short Stay," and "Two Types of People in This World."

The Dreaming Machine (Italy): "BUMPERSTICKERS."

Evening Street Review: "Other Times We Might Have Met."

43 Poems for People Who Don't Read Poetry: "The Hand of Aging Touches Some Gently."

Gargoyle Magazine: "Bird in Flight," "The Kama Sutra for Senior Citizens," and "Museum Sells Chagall Painting to Buy Minimalist Art."

Inklette: "Alstroemeria."

London Grip (UK): "Elegy for a Therapist."

Mother's Reverie, anthology from Wingless Dreamer Press (India): "What My Mother Never Told Me."

Moving Images: Poetry Inspired by Film (anthology from Before Your Quiet Eyes Publications): "Body Snatchers."

Nine Muses Poetry (UK): "No One Congratulates You" and "*Solo a Venezia*."

Phantom Kangaroo: "Where Are They Now?"

Plato's Cave (India): "I Don't Know How to Grow Old," "The Wrong Time to Bring a Child into This World," "There Are Nights When You Forget How to Sleep."

Poetica Review (UK): "Running through History" and "Soggy Jazz."

Poetry Spoken Here: "For Chaim Soutine."

Road Not Taken: "Nostalgic for Tragedy."

Saint Augustine's Magazine: "Domino Days," and "Polar Duplicates."

Superpresent Magazine: "Numerous."

About the Author

Zack Rogow is the author, editor or translator of more than twenty books and plays. His previous nine collections of poetry include *Irreverent Litanies*, *Talking with the Radio* and *The Number Before Infinity*. His memoir, *Hugging My Father's Ghost*, was released in 2024.

Zack's co-authored play, *Colette Uncensored*, had its first staged reading at the Kennedy Center in Washington DC, and later ran in London, Indonesia, Catalonia, San Francisco and Portland. His blog, *Advice for Writers*, features more than 300 posts. He has received the PEN/Book-of-the-Month Club Translation Prize, the Northern California Book Reviewers Award in Translation, and the Celestine Award for Poetry. He edited the anthology *The Face of Poetry* (University of California Press).

www.ingramcontent.com/pod-product-compliance
Ingram Content Group UK Ltd.
Pitfield, Milton Keynes, MK11 3LW, UK
UKHW040046040226
467672UK00002B/75

9 781915 606693